All About Me

MY NEIGHBORHOOD

Places and Faces

Written by Lisa Bullard • Illustrated by Brandon Reibeling

Content Advisor: Lorraine O. Moore, Ph.D., Educational Psychologist
Reading Advisor: Lauren A. Liang, M.A.
Literacy Education, University of Minnesota, Minneapolis, Minnesota

PICTURE WINDOW BOOKS
Minneapolis, Minnesota

For Sam W., who knows all about being the new kid in the neighborhood–L.B.

Designer: John Moldstad
Page production: Picture Window Books
The illustrations in this book were prepared digitally.

Picture Window Books
1710 Roe Crest Drive
North Mankato, MN 56003
www.capstonepub.com

Library of Congress Cataloging-in-Publication Data
Bullard, Lisa.
   My neighborhood : places and faces / written by Lisa Bullard;
illustrated by Brandon Reibeling.
      p. cm. — (All about me)
   Summary: Libbie gives a tour of her neighborhood to a boy just about her age whose family is moving in next door.
   ISBN-13: 978-1-4048-0047-2 (library binding)
   ISBN-10: 1-4048-0047-6 (library binding)
   ISBN-13: 978-1-4048-0162-2 (paperback)
   ISBN-10: 1-4048-0162-6 (paperback)
   [1. Neighborhood–Fiction. 2. Neighborliness–Fiction. 3. City and town life–Fiction.
4. Moving, Household–Fiction.] I. Reibeling, Brandon, ill. II. Title.
   PZ7.B91245 Myk 2003
   [Fic]–dc21
                                                        2002008546

Printed in the United States of America in North Mankato, Minnesota.
062018
000627

A new family is moving in next door. They've got a boy just my age. Mommy and I are making them cookies to welcome them to my neighborhood. In between sneaking chocolate chips, I sneak peeks at the new boy.

Finally, the cookies are done, and we go say hello. I find out the new boy's name is Michael. I tell him my name is Elizabeth but to please call me Libby.

"Why don't you show Michael around the neighborhood," Mommy says. "Just stay inside the Alone Zone." The Alone Zone is our name for how far I can walk when there isn't a grown-up with me.

The mail carrier waves to us from the sidewalk. I like it when she brings me postcards. Daddy doesn't like it when she brings bills.

Down the street, I see the Alvarezes. They are out walking their new baby, Jose. Jose can yell louder than the siren on a fire truck. We can hear him a block away!

I take Michael over to Mrs. Carlson's house, two doors down. She always tells me to visit her anytime. In the fall, I help Mrs. Carlson pick the apples off her tree. The rest of the year, I help her eat her apple pies.

The Cassidy twins like Mrs. Carlson's pies, too. I see the twins at the park across the street, so I take Michael over to play with them. Their dad has his dentist's office just two blocks away. It makes me wonder why Jack is missing two teeth and Nick is missing one.

Michael and I scramble down from the monkey bars when I see my favorite baby-sitter, Lexa. She lets me eat pizza and watch videos.

The pizza and videos come from Tony's, the corner store where Lexa works. Mommy calls it the "I-forgot store." We go there when she forgets to buy milk. Tony's is out of the Alone Zone, so Michael and I go and ask Mommy to take us there.

13

Sometimes police officers park by the store and talk with the neighbors. Mommy introduces us to Officer Higgins, but I already know him. He's been to my school to talk about staying safe.

Mommy says the officers work hard to protect us. I tell Michael I'll teach him all the safety rules.

Mommy walks with Michael and me to my favorite toy store, three blocks away. We look around and ask what's new.

Randy, the salesperson, shows us the latest science kit for rocks and minerals. He gives us each two polished rocks to take home.

Maybe next week, Mommy and I can take Michael in the car to see other places in our town, like the mall and the hospital and the library. I especially want to show him the ice cream shop.

For now, we go by the pet store and smile at the cute puppy in the window.

Michael and I have had fun exploring, but it's time to go home. Mommy wants to make her famous pot roast for dinner.

Before Michael goes inside, I tell him our next trip will be to the ice cream shop. I wave good-bye, and he knows it means, "Welcome to my neighborhood!"

Getting to Know Your Neighborhood

Activity #1: Making a Neighborhood Map

You'll need one lined sheet of paper and one large, unlined sheet of paper. You can use a pencil or crayons or markers for writing and drawing.

1. Think of all the different things you can see in your neighborhood. You might see buildings like houses, garages, apartments, stores, and schools. You might see streets or highways. You might see tall trees, water, or parks.

2. Make a list of these things on your lined sheet of paper.

3. On your large, unlined sheet of paper, draw the roads and walking paths in your neighborhood. Add any bodies of water you saw, like rivers, ponds, lakes, or ocean. Then draw the other things from your list where they fit on your map. If the school is next to the store in your neighborhood, it should be next to the store on your map.

Activity #2: Determining Your Alone Zone

1. Does your family have rules about where you can go by yourself? Where do you think your Alone Zone is?

2. Ask your mom or dad where they think your Alone Zone is. Do you agree?

3. If you don't agree, talk about why each of you feels the way you do and try to come to an agreement.

4. Mark where your Alone Zone is on your neighborhood map.

Words to Know

baby-sitter—someone hired to take care of children when their parents are away

bills—notes that are mailed to your parents telling how much money they owe

dentist—a doctor who takes care of people's teeth

hospital—a place to stay when you are sick or hurt so that doctors and nurses can take care of you

library—a place with books, magazines, and videotapes for you to borrow

mail carrier—a person who brings letters and other mail from the post office to your home

mall—a building with many stores and restaurants

neighborhood—the area around your house. The people who live in your neighborhood are your neighbors.

police officer—a person who works to keep your neighborhood safe from crime

postcard—a card with a short letter on one side and a picture on the other. People often send postcards when they are on vacation to show their friends and family the places they've visited.

sidewalk—a hard path that gives people a safe place to walk, run, or bike away from traffic

siren—a loud sound that warns people that a police car or fire truck is coming

To Learn More

At the Library

Caseley, Judith. On the Town: A Community Adventure. New York: Greenwillow Books, 2002.

DiSalvo, DyAnne. Grandpa's Corner Store. New York: HarperCollins Pub., 2000.

Dooley, Norah. Everybody Brings Noodles. Minneapolis: Carolrhoda Books, 2002.

Press, Judy. All Around Town!: Exploring Your Community Through Craft Fun. Charlotte, Vt.: Williamson Pub., 2002.

Trumbauer, Lisa. Communities. Mankato, Minn.: Yellow Umbrella Books, 2000.

On the Web

FactHound offers a safe, fun way to find Internet sites related to this book. All of the sites on FactHound have been researched by our staff.
Here's all you do:
Visit www.facthound.com
FactHound will fetch the best sites for you!